STORM BOY

WRITTEN AND ILLUSTRATED BY

Paul Owen Lewis

TRICYCLE PRESS
Berkeley, California

TRICYCLE PRESS
a little division of Ten Speed Press
P.O. Box 7123
Berkeley, California 94707
www.tenspeed.com

Design: Principia Graphica
Color: Exact Imaging

Library of Congress Catalog Card Number: 94-73364

First published in 1995 by Beyond Words Publishing
First Tricycle Press printing, 1999
First Paperback printing, 2001
ISBN 1-883672-96-1 Casebound / ISBN 1-58246-057-4 Paperback

Printed in China

3 4 5 6 7 — 08 07 06 05 04

Other Tricycle Press books by Paul Owen Lewis:
  Grasper
  Frog Girl
  Davy's Dream
  P. Bear's New Year's Party
  The Jupiter Stone

For Kyle and LeAnn

A chief's son
went fishing
alone,

and a terrible storm arose.

He soon found himself

washed ashore

under a strange sky

he had never seen before.

There was a village there.

The houses, the canoes,

and even the people

were very large.

"I am a chief's son,
and I am lost.
A storm has brought me to you,"
said the boy.
"We know this. You are welcome,
son of a chief from above,"
said one who appeared like
a chief himself.
And together they entered
the largest house of all.

Inside, the house was crowded
with finely dressed people
enjoying a feast.
They gave him a blanket to wear
and a fish to eat,
but the fish was not cut up
or cooked.

Strange, too, on the walls all around were what looked like killer whales.

After they finished eating, the chief said to the others, "Let us sing a welcome song and invite our

guest to join in the dance of our people."

"You are welcome! You are welcome! Son of a chief from above!" they sang.

The boy and his hosts began to dance around the fire together to the steady beat of the drums.

He matched them step for step, and the chief smiled
when he saw that the boy had so quickly learned
their dance.

In return, the boy offered to teach the songs and dances of his own people. The chief was delighted a now followed the boy's lead.

The celebration went on in this way for many long hours, the boy and his new friends each learning from the other.

But though the boy was enjoying himself, he began
to think more and more of home with each song he sang.

He missed his father and mother and wondered if
he would ever find his way back to them again.

Suddenly, the drumming and
dancing stopped.
The chief turned to him and said,
"We are glad that the storm has
brought you to our village,
but now you are thinking
of your own.

"When you wish to return,"
he continued, "grip my staff tightly
and stand behind me.
Close your eyes and
think of your own home,
wishing to be there only."
The boy did as he was told.
He took the staff and
stepped behind the chief.
Closing his eyes,
he pictured his father and
mother, his house, and
the people of his village.

As he did, the boy felt a great surge beneath him,
as if he were being carried upward

at greater and greater speed. He kept his eyes closed
and held on tight.

The motion stopped
and the boy opened his eyes.
There he was, lying on the beach
in front of his very own village!

"My son," cried his mother,
"where have you been? We
thought you were lost in a storm
a year ago!"

"I was lost in a storm—but it
was only yesterday!" exclaimed
the boy.

But a year's time had indeed
passed since he had disappeared
in the storm.
That night the whole village
celebrated his return and
marveled at the boy as he
danced with the staff and told
of the large and mysterious
people under the strange sky.

Common to all the world's my[...] ence renowned scholar Joseph Campbell described in three rite[...] s forth from the world of common day into a region of supernatu[...] ve victory is won: the hero comes back from this mysterious a[...] In no place is this universal theme more powerfully represen[...] Haida, Tlingit, and other Native peoples of the Northwest Coast [...]

This cosmology held that anim[...] re therefore referred to as *people*. There were wolf people, eag[...] ople. "Animals had their own territories, villages, houses, canoes[...] rm at will, blurring the distinction between animals and human[...] hen they wished to appear in their animal form they put o[...] frequently tell of heroes being escorted by spirit beings through[...] me stage betray the fact that they are really bear people or salm[...] mpbell's three rites of passage with event-motifs unique to No[...]

In an effort to present a degre[...] deliberately chosen in which the text or verbal content is spar[...] ed by the art. Therefore, for those readers interested in or unfamili[...] e and elaboration:

- *Wandering too far from the village invites supernatural encounters.*

The boy is out of sight of his village and in bad weather. His identity is indicated by the style of the canoe, which is Haida; by the text, "A chief's son"; and by his clothing—his woven cedar-bark skirt is fur-lined, a sign of wealth. Heroes were most often of high caste or rank. He is a Haida prince.

- *Mysterious entrance to the Spirit World.*

In the presence of killer whales, the boy is thrown from his canoe into the sea, passes through it, and enters into another realm below.

Northwest Coast motifs of
INITIATION

- *Animals encountered in human form.*

The grand scale of the village and the displays of killer whale crest art indicate killer whale people. The frontal pole carving indicates that it is the house of a supernatural killer whale chief—more than one dorsal fin (here there are two) indicates high rank, and the holes through the fins indicate that it is of the supernatural realm. The people are dressed in ceremonial attire, hinting that a high occasion is imminent. The boy claims his high rank as a prince and is formally welcomed by the killer whale chief.

- *Exchange of gifts and culture—"potlatching."*

Inside the house the boy notices natural killer whale forms. These are the "cloaks" that the killer whale people don to appear in the natural world. After receiving gifts of food and a blanket with a killer whale crest, the boy is taught the killer whale's dance—the most valuable of gifts and one befitting his high status. One could even argue that these are signs of his adoption by the killer whales. Dancing around the rising sparks of the cedar-wood fire, the chief punctuates this event by spreading white